MAY   2012

HEART OF EVIL

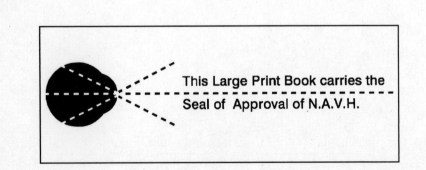

This Large Print Book carries the
Seal of Approval of N.A.V.H.

HEART OF EVIL

HEATHER GRAHAM

THORNDIKE PRESS

A part of Gale, Cengage Learning

GALE
CENGAGE Learning™

Detroit • New York • San Francisco • New Haven, Conn • Waterville, Maine • London

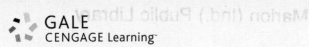

GALE
CENGAGE Learning™

LIBRARY OF CONGRESS CATALOGING-IN-PUBLICATION DATA

Graham, Heather.
    Heart of evil / by Heather Graham. — Large print ed.
        p. cm. — (Thorndike Press large print core) (Krewe of
    hunters series; 2)
    ISBN-13: 978-1-4104-3817-1
    ISBN-10: 1-4104-3817-1
    1. Supernatural—Fiction. 2. Murder—Investigation—Fiction.
    3. New Orleans (La.)—Fiction. 4. Large type books. I. Title.
    PS3557.R198H43 2011
    813'.54—dc22   2011014018

Published in 2011 by arrangement with Harlequin Books S.A.

Printed in the United States of America
1 2 3 4 5 6 7 15 14 13 12 11

Dedicated with gratitude
to the beautiful Myrtles plantation,
and to Teeta LeBleu Moss, owner,
Teresa David, the General Manager,
Hester Eby, Director of Tours,
Taryn Lowery, Tour Guide
and to Scout and Sprout
and The Peace River Ghost Trackers

And to Dennis, Jason, Shayne,
and Bryee-Annon Pozzessere;
Teresa Davant, Kathy Pickering,
Kathy DePalo, Juan Roca,
Bridget LeVien, Matthew Green,
Phinizy Percy Jr., and Connie Perry.

PROLOGUE

Blood.

She could see it, smell it.

Hear it.

Drip . . . drip . . . drip . . .

The air was heavy with black powder, and the brilliant red color of the blood seemed to form a mist with the powder, and she was surrounded by a haze, a miasma of gray-tinged crimson. The day was dying, becoming red, red like the color of the blood seeping to the ground, making that terrible, distinctive noise. Drip, drip, drip . . .

Ashley Donegal was there. She wasn't even sure where *there* was, but she knew that she didn't want to be there.

Suddenly, the mist seemed to swirl in a violent gust, and then settle softly, closer to the ground. It parted as she walked through. She could see her surroundings, and, at that moment, she knew. She was in the cemetery.

She had played here so often as a child — respectfully, of course. Her grandfather never would have had it any other way. Those elegant tombs, all constructed with such love, and an eye to the priorities of the day. The finest craftsmen had been hired, artists and artisans, and the place was truly beautiful. Angels and archangels graced the various tombs, winged cherubs, saints and crosses. She had never been afraid.

But now . . .

From a distance, she could hear shouts. Soldiers. Ridiculous. Grown men playing as soldiers. But they did it so well. She might almost have been back in time. The powder came from the howitzer and the Enfield rifles. The shouts sounded as the men played out their roles, edging from the river road to the outbuildings and then the stables, to the final confrontation on the lawn and in the cemetery. The blood would come from stage packets within their uniforms, of course, but . . .

This was *real* blood. She knew because it had a distinctive odor, and because, yes, damn it, she could *smell* it. Nothing smelled like real blood.

She looked at the ground, and she could see the puddle where the blood was falling, but she was afraid to look up. If she looked up, she would see a dead man.

But she did so anyway. She saw him. There was a hat pulled low over his face, but soon he would lift his head.

He did. And she saw a man in his prime, handsome, with strength of purpose in the sculpture of his face. But there was weariness in his eyes.

Weariness and death. Yet they were just playacting; that past was so, so long ago now. . . .

She didn't speak. Neither did he. Because his face began to rot. It blackened, and while she watched, the scabrous decaying flesh began to peel away. Soon she was staring into the empty eye sockets of a skull.

She started to scream.

Above that sound, she could hear someone calling to her. Someone calling her name. The sound was deep, rich and masculine, and she knew it. . . .

It was Jake! He would help. . . . Surely he would help.

But she could only stare at the skeletal mask in front of her.

Smell the blood.

And scream.

A strange sound in the middle of the night awoke Ashley. She sat up with a start and realized she was doing the screaming. She clamped her own hand quickly over her mouth, embarrassed and praying that she hadn't roused the household. She waited in silence; nope, no one.

That was pretty pathetic. It must have been a horrifically pathetic scream. If she ever really needed to scream, she'd probably be out of luck.

Lord, that had been some nightmare.

She didn't *have* nightmares. She was the most grounded human being she knew; hell, she had grown up next to a bayou full of alligators and cottonmouths, and she had lived in a downtrodden area of New York City near Chinatown in order to afford NYU. She knew all about *real* monsters — ghosts were creations to reel tourists in.

So . . .

With a groan, she threw her head back on her pillow and glanced at the clock. She needed to sleep. In a week's time, they'd be celebrating Donegal Plantation's biggest annual event: the reenactment of the skirmish here that had cost her ancestor his life.

Ah, yes, and she had been dreaming about the skirmish — or the reenactment?

That was it, she thought, grinning. She was dreaming about the events at Donegal

Plantation because they were preparing for the day.

History was always alive at Donegal. The plantation house was furnished with antiques, most of which had been in the family forever. There was an attic room that contained more artifacts from the Civil War than many a museum, down to letters, mess kits, knapsacks, pistols, rifles and bayonets. Still, the reenactment remained a major undertaking.

But they'd been running it since before she had even been born. It was rote by now. All the same, there was still plenty of bustle and confusion, along with everything that had to happen before the event could take place, including a mound of paperwork on her desk that had to do with the "sutler's tent," the pop-up shop where period clothing and curios and other paraphernalia, such as weapons and antiques, were sold. Which meant registrations and taxes. Then there was the insurance they needed for the day, and the officers to direct traffic and so on.

That was it. She just had a lot on her mind.

And the reenactment always reminded her of Jake. He'd never been a soldier, North or South. But he'd dressed up, and he'd played his guitar and sang music from the era. And sometimes she had played with him, and he'd always known how to make it just right, to bring back the past, with the light of truth.

She eased down in her covers, determined to forget both her anxiety and Jake.

Not so easy, even though it had been a long time since Jake had been in her life.

Finally, she started to drift again. She was comfortable; she loved her bed and her room, even if she had lived here her whole life other than college. Though she loved to learn about new people and new places, she also loved to be home.

She started again, certain that she had felt a touch; something soft and gentle, smoothing her hair, stroking her cheek.

She sat up. Moonlight streamed into the room, and there was no one else here; with so many guests around, she had locked her bedroom door. She looked at her pillow and decided that she had merely rubbed against a side of the pillowcase.

As she did so, she glanced at her dresser.

There was something different about it. She studied it for a moment, wondering what it was.

Then she knew.

She kept a picture of her parents there, on

her dresser. It had been taken almost twenty years ago. They were together, holding her between them, when she had been five. It had been developed in sepia tone, and they'd had it done when one of the guests at a reenactment had found a way of making nice money by pretending to be Matthew Brady, the famed Civil War photographer. Throughout the day, he had answered historical questions about photography and its place in the Civil War.

As was the custom of the day, none of them was smiling, but there was still something exceptionally charming about the picture. There was a light in her father's eyes, and just the hint of a curl at her mother's lips. Her father's arm was around her, his hand coming to rest tenderly on her mother's shoulder. She was sandwiched close between them, and in her mind, the picture had been filled with love. It had become an even greater treasure when she had lost them.

It usually faced at a slight angle toward her bed.

The picture was turned away, as if someone had been looking at it from a different angle. It was such a little thing, but . . .

Maybe someone had wandered into her room. Cliff ran the property and she ran

13

the house, but they employed extra house-keepers in the main house when they had guests. They hadn't had guests *in* the house in the last few weeks, but the house was usually open, and her grandfather loved to walk anyone staying on the property through it. Depending on his mood, a tour could get long.

And the picture . . .

She turned over, groaning. It was just the angle of the picture.

Jake Mallory should have slept well, with a hard case finally settled.

But he didn't.

The odd thing about his nightmares was that they were a recent phenomenon. When he had begun to realize and make use of this gift or curse — those things he somehow *knew* — there had been no dreams.

During the summer of the storms, during Katrina and the flooding, they had all been so busy. While it had been happening, he'd never explained to his coworkers that he was so good at finding the remains of the deceased because they called out to him; they spoke to him. It was heartbreaking; it was agony. But the dead needed their loved ones to know, and so he listened. And he didn't dream those nights.

Later, the dreams had come, and they were always the same.

He was alone in his small, flat-bottomed boat, though he'd never been alone during any of the searches.

He was alone, and the heat of the day had cranked down to the lesser heat of the night, and he was searching specifically for someone, though he didn't know who. As the boat moved through the water that should have been a street, he began to see people on the rooftops, clinging to branches here and there, and even floating in the water.

They saw him; they reached out to him. And he felt like weeping. They weren't living people. They were those who had lost the fight.

As he drifted along, he looked back at them all, men and women, old and young, black and white and all colors in between. He wanted to ease their suffering, but he could no longer save them. Their faces had an ashen cast, and the bone structure was sucked in and hollow; they didn't seem to know that there was nothing he could do for them anymore. In the dream, he knew that he, like many law-enforcement officers, scent dogs and volunteers, would be called upon to find the dead in the future.

But now he was seeking the living.

They called out to him; they were trying to tell him something. Bit by bit, he saw they were trying to show him the way. He thought that there should have been sound, but there was none. He didn't hear his passage through the water, and nothing emitted from the mouths of the corpses he passed.

Then he saw the figure on the roof far ahead. He thought it was a woman. She seemed to be in something flowing, which was not unusual. Many victims, living and dead, had been found in nightgowns or boxers or flannel pajamas. What was strange was that she seemed to be the only one alive. She was in tremendous peril as the water rose all around her. He felt that there was something familiar about her, but he didn't understand what it was that seemed to touch him. The light of the full moon turned her hair golden and gleaming, her white gown flowed in the breeze. Amidst the destruction, she was a beautiful survivor.

He tried to get closer.

The watery road grew more clogged and congested. Downed tree branches and appliances floated by. A soaked teddy bear with big black button eyes stared at him sightlessly as it drifted. He ached inside; it was an agony to fight the river, but it was also something he knew he had to do. Especially when *she* waited; when he could save her. He just had to reach her before the water level rose higher and higher, and swept her away.

He grew close . . .

And that was when he felt the darkness at his back.

He tried to turn, but he could not. The wind had picked up, and the effort was too much. No matter how he strained, he couldn't see what evil thing seemed to be tracking him.

There was suddenly sound. The woman. She was calling out to him.

She called him by name.

But he could feel the thing behind him gaining on him. He could almost reach out for her, but he had to turn, had to find out what seemed to be breathing fetid air down his back. . . .

She called out again.

Jake!

If they were to survive, to outrun whatever horror was behind him, they would have to do so together.

Jake!

Her voice rang out almost as clearly as if she were next to him in the boat.

But the darkness was on him, so close. . . .

He could feel it then, enveloping him, crushing the sound of her voice as it did.

And he woke with a jerk.

Jake sat up in bed, deeply disturbed by the reappearance of his frequent dream. For the first time, he knew who he had seen on the roof of the house, about to be swallowed up by the floodwaters.

It was Ashley. Ashley Donegal.

He stood and stretched, irritated. The clock on his mantel indicated it was still early.

He swore and got dressed. He knew why he'd had the dream — and made Ashley the woman on the rooftop. He knew the date. The reenactment was coming. Donegal Plantation would be busy and alive; Ashley would still hurt from the fact that her dad had passed away and would no longer be playing Marshall Donegal, his ancestor. But she'd never show it. She'd be the grand mistress of the ceremonies, beautiful and regal in her Civil War attire.

He wondered if he would ever fall out of love with her. And then he wondered if the dream had meant something more. Angela — who seemed to have the best sixth sense in what the FBI called their special unit — had told him that dreams could open many

18

doors. In REM sleep, the mind was at the stage where dreams came, and those dreams could easily focus on what the conscious mind rejected. When she was trying to reach memories of the past, she often used sleep.

If that were the guide, he could easily convince himself to think that Ashley now wanted him. Needed him. And that this was the sign.

Of course, that was just Angela's way of seeking the ghosts of the past — even in their own group, they weren't sure about all the rules of seeking out the help of ghosts.

He wasn't sure if he wanted to laugh at himself or not.

Their team was legitimate; they were on-the-books federal agents. They had just spent days at the local training facility, improving their weapons skills, computer literacy and understanding of the mission policy.

But they were a one-of-a-kind unit, and their true designation wasn't written down anywhere. Among themselves, they were the Krewe of Hunters; on paper, they were Adam Harrison's Special Unit. In bizarre situations, they were supposed to smoke out the fakers — and find what might really be remnants of the past.

The world was filled with ghost hunters

and would-be ghost hunters. The problem that most people didn't see was the fact that few ghosts would really appear for a television crew. Some ghost lore did seem to be true. There were the residual hauntings — ghosts that played out a situation, such as a battle scene at Gettysburg, over and over again. And there were intelligent hauntings: ghosts that lingered for some reason. Ghosts didn't seem to have rules. Some could find certain individuals who saw them as clearly as day; they could carry on long conversations, appear and disappear, and interact. Sometimes ghosts were frightened of the living, and they hid, and only someone with a real ability to suspend disbelief could coax them out. It was complicated; he was still learning. Sometimes ghosts tried to warn those they cared about when something evil was about to occur, and ghosts often entered into the REM sleep of those they hadn't managed yet to really touch in the conscious world.

So the dream meant that Ashley needed him. . . .

Or he wanted the dream to mean that Ashley needed him.

He stood up and walked over to his hotel window and looked out over the dark streets of the French Quarter. There was so much history here. So many lives had been lived; so much drama had taken place. Sometimes it was impossible to believe that the energy of the past *didn't* remain. Ghosts didn't have to be old; he knew that himself, though he hadn't wanted to accept the truth until he had met Adam Harrison and become a part of the unit Adam had started for the FBI. He had been glad of his ability to *feel* where people were; to imagine that he heard them telling him to come, please. Sometimes he had even been able to find the living. And sometimes he had heard the voices of the dead, when he hadn't known that they were dead.

His "gift" had cost him Ashley.

So why now, all these years later, was he seeing her, adrift, about to be engulfed, and yet reaching for him, even as he reached for her?

1

"Ah, dammit! I don't want to be a Yankee," Charles Osgood said.

It was there; it had finally come, and Ashley was grateful.

And the semi-drama going on here surely meant her mind had been trying to warn her that the day was not going to come without its share of trouble, because it was already proving to be one hell of an afternoon.

Morning had brought the business of breakfast, visitors pouring onto the property to spend time at the campsites. Now they were coming close to the main event of the day, the reenactment of the battle that had taken place at Donegal Plantation.

She'd never expected the real trouble to come over the sad situation of an ailing faux-Yankee.

"Dammit!" Charles exclaimed again.

Ashley thought that the man sounded like

23

a petulant teenager, though she knew that he didn't really want to argue. Not on a day like today. He flushed as the words came out of his mouth, and cast her a quick glance of dismay. She wasn't even the one handing out the assignments, though she was the only Donegal among them now. The relish the group was taking in telling Charles his new role unsettled her a bit. Charles Osgood was the newest in the "cavalry unit" of reenactors, which meant that he got the assignment to play for the other side. Yet this seemed to be turning into a college hazing; they were all friends, and they were usually courteous to one another.

"Charlie, come on! Being a Yankee will be fun. Okay, so they were jerks — well, the ones here — who couldn't spy on a neon sign, couldn't hunt, couldn't shoot. . . . But come on! Being a Yank will be fun!" Griffin Grant teased.

Ashley shook her head; how could grown men be so immature?

In *her* mind, although she truly loved the living history that took place at the plantation, she thought the units clinging to so-called glory were nothing more than inane. The event had ended with the *death* of one her ancestors — not a party.

"Hey, hey, all of you!" Ashley said, addressing the men around her and using the voice she would utilize when working with one of the school groups — the grade-school groups. "I know you all like to cling to the magical illusion that the antebellum South was a place of beauty, grace and honor — where men were men. Real men, hunting, riding, brawling — but honorable. Yes, we reenact what was. But this is now, and that was then! None of you would seriously want to go back to the Civil War, and no one here is prejudiced. The slavery of any person was a horrendous way of life."

"Ashley — you're making it sound like being a real man is bad thing!" Cliff Boudreaux commented, laughing. Cliff, horse master at Donegal, was clearly amused and having a good time.

"Well, of course, Ashley, it's not like we take this too seriously," Griffin Grant said, staring back at her as if she was the one who didn't understand the question. Griffin was a striking man in his early thirties, sleek and slick, a CEO for a cable company in New Orleans, though his ancestors had lived out here, two hours down the road from the big city. "We know reality — and like it. But this is important playacting!"

She groaned softly.

They were good guys, really.

It was playacting, and for the playacting they were able to believe truly with their whole hearts that it had been about nothing other than states' rights. Ashley knew all the statistics about the fighting men — most of the men who fought and died for the South during the war couldn't have begun to have afforded a slave — and war was seldom caused by one issue. But her parents and her grandfather had never been the types to overlook the plantation's complicated history. Cliff was part of that with his gold-green eyes, bronze-colored skin and dark tawny hair. She knew that half their visitors were immediately enthralled with him. He was one of the reenactors on the Southern side because of the Donegal blood that ran in his veins. Early on, a Donegal widower had fallen in love with a slave, creating the first racial mix in his background. In the 1920s, his great-grandfather had married a Donegal cousin, something that caused a serious scandal at that time in history, but which now gave both halves of the family a sense of pleasure and pride. She wasn't sure how to count second and third or twice-removed relatives, so she considered Cliff to be her cousin.

History was history. Donegal was steeped in it, good and bad, and they didn't hide any of it.

"Charles, they're right. It's a performance, you know," Ashley said. "It's a show, maybe even an important show in its small way. It's where people can see the weapons of the day, the uniforms that were worn. And, actually, remember, this particular fight started because men had a bar brawl — and then an excuse to fight because the war was getting underway. You're all examples of keeping history alive, and I'm so grateful to all of you."

Charles stared back at her blankly; the other men were smirking.

Why didn't they all get it? They were actors in a show, hopefully teaching American history, with several perspectives, along the way. But some things died really slowly here, in plantation country. Family was still everything. Loyalty to hearth and home, kin, parish and state. They'd been wrong; they'd been beaten, and they knew it, but still, only one side of the cast of players was considered to be elite. And the reenactors could be incredibly snobbish.

That made Charles Osgood the odd man out.

Toby Keaton cleared his throat and then said softly, "Charles — come on. You're lucky to be in with the 27th Bayou Militia

Cavalry Unit. Most of the time, the fellows taking part in the reenactments here are direct descendants of those who fought before. You've got to see the truth of this thing. You claim your place in the ranks through marriage — your stepfather was an O'Reilly, and I know he raised you, but, you know, in other old Southern units, that wouldn't count." Toby was forty-four, and Ashley's next-door neighbor at Beaumont, his Creole plantation, though they both had acres and acres of land. Toby grinned as if to cut the harshness of his words. "Newcomer — odd man out. You're a Yankee if I've ever seen one!"

"Great! So now I'm a newcomer — and that makes me an outsider?" Charles asked, staring around the room. "Come on, guys, you've just got to understand. This will really make it look as if I don't belong here at all!"

He gave his appeal to the others gathered at the horse master's office in the old barn at Donegal Plantation that day — Cliff Boudreaux, Griffin Grant, Toby Keaton, Ramsay Clayton, Hank Trebly, all still with property in the general area, John Ashton, tour director from New Orleans, and Ashley herself. The "Yankees" were gathering in the old smokehouse — a separate building, and now a small apartment. Charles would be joining them soon; all of the reenactors gathered together for their roundtable discussions on the war, but each side met separately first on the day of the reenactment to make sure that every member knew the character he was playing. Later, they'd all meet back here to make sure that everyone was apprised of all the safety factors involved.

One, Charles, so it seemed, would have to play a Yankee, and go join the group in the apartment. They were short a Yankee, and that's the way it was. All of them belonged to Civil War roundtables, and these days, none of them really cared about sides — they just liked to discuss tactics and procedure. They often met in the dining room at Donegal; Ashley loved to listen, because they also knew their history, and they spoke about events in the lives of many of the key players in the war, and the fact that the generals had often been best friends before they had been forced to choose sides in the bloody conflict. They knew about weapons, uniforms, sad stories about treason and resisters, draft riots, food, clothing, trade and so much more.

"Charles," Cliff Boudreaux said patiently. "We're all just teasing you here, really. We're short on Yankees today, on account of Barton Waverly being sick with the flu. We're pretty desperate. And that's the rule; newcomers play Yankees when our brothers from up North ask for help. Hell, remember that year when half of us were laid up with the croup? Three of them Yankees had to come play Southern boys. We're not doing anything bad to you — really."

Ramsay Clayton was seated across the table from Cliff. Ramsay looked like an artist; he was tall, with a wiry muscle structure, long dark hair and classical features. He owned a small place down the road, but he spent a lot of time in New Orleans, where he sometimes showed his work at Jackson Square and sometimes had showings at the galleries. He grinned at Charles. "Yeah, and don't forget, the Yankees won. Hell, come to think about it, where were all the Southern boys when we were losing this thing?" he asked lightly. "Ah, well. Born in our day and age, it's easy to look back at the South's part in the Civil War and wonder, 'What the hell were we thinking?' "

Ashley smiled. She liked Ramsay. He was a good guy.

"Well, I wish I could just step up to the plate, but I can't. I can't play a Yankee — I just can't," Toby Keaton said. "Hell, my great-great-great-whatever grandfather was the first one to answer Marshall Donegal's call for volunteers. He was one of his best friends. I think he'd roll in his grave if I played a Yankee. Good God! I own a plantation! Wouldn't be fitting for me to play a Yankee. Lord knows, it could be bad for business."

Hank Trebly grinned. "Well, I'm just big sugar. I don't really give a whit. I see the war as over, over, over, and that's the way it is. Lord A-mighty! The damn thing ended in 1865." Hank owned the property next to Donegal, and his ancestors had owned it forever. The old plantation had been replaced by a sugar refinery years ago. He was a small man, in his early forties, and his business meant everything to him.

John Ashton shrugged. "My family might have been here, but I don't care," he said. "The Civil War means my income these days — tourists love to go back. But I love 'em all. Yankees, rebels, Brits, Brazilians! Bring them on. They all spend money and take tours."

"And what happened here was in 1861, for God's sake, before the thing had really even gotten going," Griffin said, shaking his head. "Come on, now! My ancestor went on to die at the Second Battle of Manassas

— now, that's a damned big battle. We're here to teach, and to remember everything that happened in the past — and how it made us what we are today. Let's have fun, folks. C'mon — I come out here to forget the office and programming and statistics, computers and red tape. I don't care who plays what. It's just for a good time."

"I spend most of my time in New Orleans, art on the square and all that — you can call me a doughboy for all I care. It's the spirit of this thing," Ramsay said. "And Lord knows, what happened here couldn't even be called a battle. My ancestor and most of the Southern boys except for Marshall survived, but, as we've all pointed out now — the North won. We are living in the United States of America. This wasn't even really a battle."

He was right. What had taken place late in 1861 hadn't even been a battle. Drinking downriver, toward New Orleans, two Yankee spies had heard about Donegal's then-owner — Marshall Donegal — preparing a major summons to area troops to prepare them for an invasion of New Orleans. In trying to draw Marshall Donegal's men out further on the subject, they had all gotten into a fistfight when one made a ridiculous statement about Northerners being chickens. The two Confederates suspected the men of being spies, and had run back to Donegal. The spies went back to their headquarters, but they were *spies,* and thus their numbers were small. On each side, six men were mustered — and, rather than be executed as spies if they were caught, the Union men donned their uniforms.

The fighting had ranged from the stables to the porch of the main house and out to the chapel and cemetery — ending when Captain Marshall Donegal had died of a bayonet wound in his own family graveyard. The enemy had "skedaddled," according to the Southern side; the rebels had been left in utter defeat, according to their Northern counterparts.

Now, the "battle" was something that taught history, and, largely due to its small size — and the fact that the current owner of the plantation, Ashley's grandfather, Frazier Donegal, was a history buff and glad to welcome the units on his property — it was a popular event. "Living history" took place frequently at Donegal, as often as once a week, but an actual reenactment was done only once a year. Sometimes the actors doing the reenactments were involved in other locations. Some belonged not just to Civil War units, but Revolutionary War units, and it just depended on where the biggest shin-dig was going on. Luckily, most of the men who could claim to have had ancestors in the brawl loved the plantation and the nearly exact-to-the-past-moment location of the place, and they usually made this reenactment a priority.

Donegal House was surely one of the prettiest places left on the river road, with memories of the antebellum era held in place. The great house still maintained a gorgeous front. It had been built with magnificent Greek columns and wrap-around porches, and elegant tree-shaded entries stretched forever before the front and back doors. The currently used stables, housing only six horses, were next to the house, while the larger stables needed in a bygone era were far back from the house, to the left, riverside, and offered three apartments for those who wanted to stay for the night. The old smokehouse and servants' quarters were available for rent as well, and sometimes they even rented out five of the rooms in the main house. With Beth there, Ashley's extraordinarily talented friend and chef, and the efforts they were making with the restaurant and the crazy business that came along with the reenactment, they had chosen this year just to let rooms in the outbuildings.

All this — living history and their bed-and-breakfast rentals — was done to survive into the twenty-first century. But the Donegal family had been letting the place out for nearly thirty years now. And the living history and the reenactments were the true highlights to be found here, distinguishing it from other great plantations along the river.

"Okay, sure. You all are right," Charles said. "It's over. Long over. Hell, the Yankees did win the war."

Cliff laughed. "Still hard to convince my mama and a few other folks I know that it's true. But thanks, Charles, that's great. The Yanks are good guys. Man, it's sad to think back, though, huh? We would have wound up being enemies."

"Who knows what our feelings would have been back then?" Ashley asked. "We might have chosen to fight for the North."

"It was a different time, a different life-style," Griffin pointed out. "You're all indignant now about injustice, but you didn't live back then. You didn't grow up in an economy of cotton and sugar."

"Rich men wanted to stay rich," Ramsay agreed dryly.

"Who's being Marshall Donegal today?"

Charles asked.

"That would be me," Ramsay said. "I've done it the past five years." He was quiet a minute; he had done it since Ashley's father had passed away. "Ashley could don a uniform herself, but she thinks we boys should just be boys. So I get the honor."

Ramsay was trying to move quickly past the mention of her father, Ashley knew. He had been gone five years now; he had died shortly after her mother. She had accepted their loss — and she knew as well that there would still be a little core of pain when she thought about them, even if she lived to be one hundred. Inwardly, she winced. She hadn't just lost her father that day; that had been the end of her and Jake. Her fault, her call, and she still wasn't sure why. He had frightened her, she thought. It seemed he had scratched the surface of something, and she didn't want to know what was beneath. And still, to this day, she knew that although she had closed the door, she missed Jake. And missing Jake had colored everything else in her life.

"He died," Charles reminded him. "Marshall Donegal was killed, you know," he added quickly.

"Well, as we've said, the war is long over, so I guess they're all dead now anyway,"

36

Ramsay pointed out.

"Gentlemen," Ashley said, speaking at last, "I want you all to know that you are greatly appreciated. You're all such wonderful actors, taking on whatever role is needed, whenever it's needed! Charles, the Yankees are great guys. Michael Bonaventure lives in town, and his ancestors lived there as well, right in the heart of the French Quarter. His family left when the war started, because Bonaventure's ancestor was fighting for the Union. Hadley Mason is from Lafayette, but his ancestors agreed with the Northern cause as well. It will be fun for you to be a Yankee. It's acting, just like when we act out the encampments. And I truly appreciate you taking on the role."

"It's really amazing," Griffin said. "We do get all tied up in what *was*. The way the past still has so much to do with the present! Charles, come on, you're a *stepchild*. We all really had ancestors back then who were involved with this thing. You're welcome among us — totally welcome. But, hey, if I had come in on this recently, I'd be happy just to be a part of it all."

Charles Osgood offered Ashley a weak smile. "Sure. You know me — I'm just happy to be here."

To Ashley's surprise, Ramsay Clayton

suddenly spoke up again. "Charles, I have an idea. Some of those guys really are my friends. My good friends. I'll be a Yankee today. You be Marshall Donegal."

Charles opened his mouth, stunned, and stared at Ramsay. "Oh! Oh, no. I couldn't take that honor away from you!"

"You get killed, you know," Ramsay reminded him.

"Oh, like you said, they're all dead now. I just couldn't — I really couldn't."

"Hey, I think I want to be a Yankee for once," Ramsay said. "It's cool. You be Marshall Donegal, and I'll be a Yankee. No arguments — it's decided. I'll be a winner for a change!"

"I don't know what to say!" Charles told him.

"Say thanks, and let's get on with it. We have to finish planning this thing," Ramsay said.

"I'm going to be Marshall Donegal!" Charles said, still awed.

Ashley lowered her head, hiding her laughter. These guys really were like children when it came to the reenactment. They were so dedicated. But it was really good, she reminded herself. They kept history alive. It had been on a trip to Europe with her parents when she had seen the quote that

38

meant so much to her: "Those who cannot remember the past are condemned to repeat it." It was the philosopher George Santayana who had written those words, and she had seen them above the gates of a concentration camp. So, whether history was sterling or not — pitting man at his best and his worst — it was necessary to remember.

The reenactors did a fantastic job. Although there had been only a small encampment at Donegal Plantation at the time, they recreated a larger one, complete with a medical tent, where surgeries were acted out, officers' quarters and tents for enlisted men.

"This is a right nice place to meet, but we need to get to business," Griffin said, winking at Ashley.

"Yeah, Ramsay, looks like you need to skedaddle!" Cliff teased.

"I'm out of here!" Ramsay said, rising. He looked around. "Sadly, I do like Cliff's digs better than being cramped up in an apartment!"

Griffin was right: they *were* in a nice place to meet. The office/living quarters in the stables were extremely pleasant; there was no heavy smell of hay, horses or droppings in any way, since the office had long ago been fitted out with air-conditioning and an air purifier to boot. There were a number of trophies along with books on horses, horse care, tack and maps on the shelves around the old massive desk with its iMac and printer. It was the horse master's realm. No matter the state of riches or poverty the Donegal Plantation might be in, there was always a horse master. These days, the horse master did more than look after the six horses that remained. He was a tour guide, overseer — though they didn't grow anything other than a few flowers now and then and a tomato plant or two — and general man about the house.

Ashley stood and gave him a shove. "Our apartments are beautiful. Get on out of here, and get this all moving!" She spoke with teasing force. "I'm going out to check on the camp setup and see that everything is running smoothly, then get ready. I'll leave you gentlemen to agree on the final assignments and action. The day is moving on. We need to be prepared to start with the battle at sundown."

"Hell, I hope they got a uniform that will fit me!" He winked. Ramsay was a good guy. He had a small house that had once been a working plantation, but his land had been eaten up over the years. Plantation actually meant farm, and Ramsay had no farmland left at all. He spent most of his time in the city, where he actually was a working artist making a nice income.

"I'm off to join the Yankees!"

"Thanks!" Charles Osgood lifted a hand to Ramsay, and then to Ashley, looking dazed. He was getting the prime role for the day, and he still seemed to be surprised.

It didn't mean as much to Ramsay, Ashley thought, watching him as he walked from the stables to the old barn. He was from here; he'd been born a part of it all. He'd played soldiers over and over again, and though it had been magnanimous of him to hand over the role, she wasn't sure that Ramsay hadn't decided that being a Yankee might not be that bad a thing for the day. After all, they ended the day with the Pledge of Allegiance and the "Battle Hymn of the Republic." Even if they did begin it with a rousing chorus of "Dixie"!

She left Cliff's to make a quick check of the horses. "Thank God you darlings don't care if you're Yankees or rebels!" she said affectionately, pausing to rub Abe's ears. She saw that the tack for the Northern cavalry was ready for each of the mounts, saddles and saddle blankets set on sawhorses and the bridles with their insignias hanging from hooks right outside the stalls. Abe, Jeff, Varina, Tigger, Nellie and Bobby were all groomed and sleekly beautiful, ready to play their parts. She paused to give Varina a pat; she loved all the horses, but Varina was her special mare, the horse she always chose to ride.

Leaving the stables, Ashley paused for a moment to look across the expanse of acreage to the left, where the tents of the living encampment had been set up. She could see the sutler's stretch of canvas, and she walked over to see who was working that day. Tourists — parked way down the river road — were milling around the goods for sale. She heard children squealing with delight as they discovered toys from the mid-nineteenth century, just as she heard women ooh and aah over some of the corsets and clothing. She saw that a crowd had gathered around the medical tent where reenactors were doing a spectacular job of performing an amputation. The patient let out a horrific scream, and then passed out. Dr. Ben Austin — playing his ancestor, also Dr. Ben Austin — stood in an apron covered in stage blood and explained the procedure. Ben would later be part of the battle reenactment, but for now, he was explaining medicine. Ashley reached him in time to

42

capture part of his spiel.

"Amputation was frequently the only choice for a Civil War surgeon, and field surgeons could perform an amputation in as little as ten minutes," Ben told the crowd. "Chloroform existed, but it was scarce. The South had alcohol. When the surgeon could, he would do everything in his power to make the traumatic operation easier for his patient, but at major battles, the pile of amputated limbs could easily grow to be five feet tall. There was no real understanding of germs, and more men died from disease than from wounds or bullets. To carry that further, more men died in the Civil War than in any other American war, and more men died at Sharpsburg, or Antietam, as those of you from the North might know it, than died during the D-Day invasion."

Ben saw Ashley watching him and lifted a bloody hand. Well, it was covered in faux blood from the faux surgery. Ben knew how to be dramatic. She smiled and waved in return and went on, stopping to chat with some of the women who were cooking, darning or sewing at the living-encampment tents. There were soldiers around as well, explaining Enfield rifles to little boys, whittling, playing harmonicas or engaging in other period activities. One laundress was hanging shirts and long johns out to dry — a nice touch, Ashley thought.

"When the war started, the North already had a commissary department — and the South didn't," Matty, the sutler's wife, was explaining to a group who stood around the campfire she had nurtured throughout the day. "Hardtack — dried biscuits, really — molasses, coffee, sugar, salted beef or pork and whatever they could scrounge off the land was what fed the soldiers, and the South had to scramble to feed the troops. Didn't matter how rich you were — you were pretty much stuck with what could be gotten. There were points, especially at the beginning of the war, during which the Southern soldiers were doing all right. They were on Southern soil. But war can strip the land. What I'm doing here is boiling salted beef and trying to come up with something like a gravy to soften up the hardtack. With a few precious spices, salt and sugar, it won't be too bad. A few people can taste, if they like! Of course, I've made sure that our hardtack has no boll weevils. The soldiers were fighting every kind of varmint, big and small, to keep their own food."

Everything seemed to be in perfect order; Ashley's dreams had been for nothing.